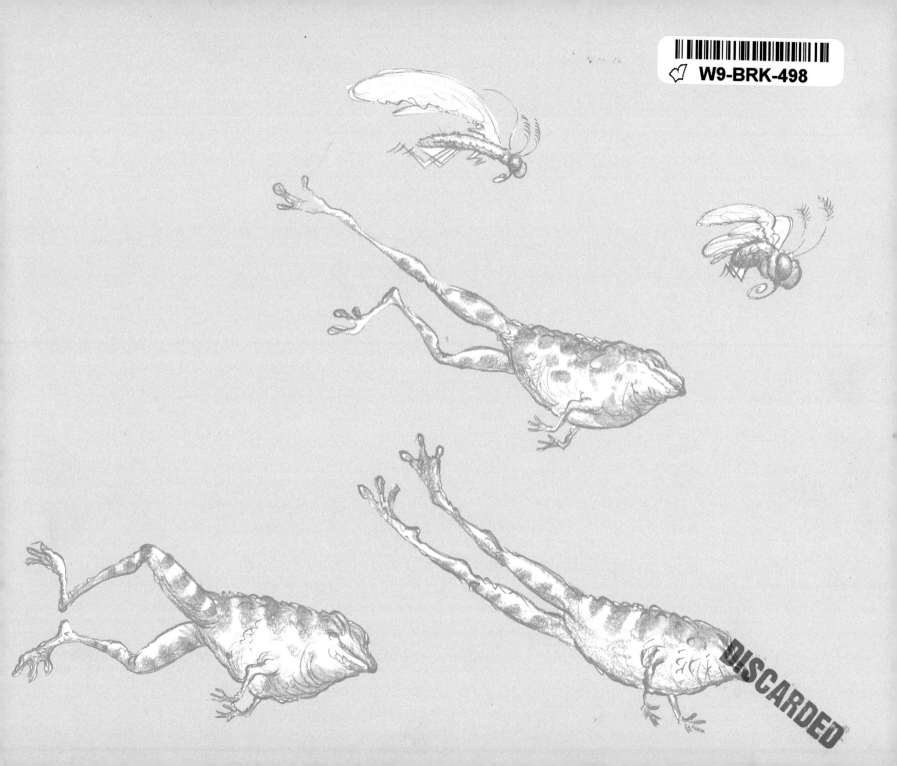

# Dozens _of_ Cousins

by SHUTTA CRUM    Illustrated by DAVID CATROW

CLARION BOOKS

Houghton Mifflin Harcourt • Boston  New York • 2013

Clarion Books
215 Park Avenue South
New York, New York 10003

Text copyright © 2013 by Shutta Crum
Illustrations copyright © 2013 by David Catrow

Clarion Books is an imprint of Houghton Mifflin Harcourt Publishing Company.

www.hmhbooks.com

The text was set in 16-point Cooper Old Style.
The illustrations were executed in pencil, ink, and gouache.

Book design by Kerry Martin

Library of Congress Cataloging-in-Publication Data
Crum, Shutta.
Dozens of cousins / by Shutta Crum ; illustrated by David Catrow.
p. cm.
Summary: At a family reunion, dozens of "beastie" cousins spend the day running wild,
playing in the creek, filling up on food, and making mischief.
ISBN 978-0-618-15874-4
[1. Family reunions—Fiction. 2. Cousins—Fiction. 3. Behavior—Fiction.] I. Catrow, David, ill. II. Title.
PZ7.C888288Doz 2013
[E]—dc23
2012005010

Manufactured in China
SCP 10 9 8 7 6 5 4 3 2 1
4500403858

For my lovable "beastie" cousins: Jack, Larry, and Garry Crum—
what fun we had! —S.C.

To Aunt Hedie, Aunt Olive, Aunt Mildred,
and Gramma Flo—D.C.

4

OH, we are hungry ogres, my cousins and I.
As kinfolks gather once again,
we spill out of cars,
snatch up greetings, stuff ourselves
on hellos and howdys.
A beastie family reunion!

5

With beastie courage we greet our aunt
who grabs for us and says, "Glory be!"
With beastie paws we tackle our uncles
who tickle us and say, "Good golly!"

With bare arms, bare legs, bare feet,
we race through the world,
snatching it up and eating it,
running with hearts hungry for hugs
and tummies hungry for treats.
Yummy beastie food!

7

We are wild and fierce.
We do not wait for invitations.
We run through front doors, arms extended,
slap dirty feet on cool linoleum,
grab from plates thrust out at us—and holler for more.

9

Oh, we are rowdy ogres.
We roar! We growl!
We parade out back doors and leap over steps,
rushing down to the secret grottoes of the creek.

10

We fill up on beastie delights—
on catching frogs and crawdads,
on double-dog dares crossing balancing logs,
and on tales the water mumbles
as it tumbles along.

11

We grow bolder.
Everything is good.
Everything is luscious.
We are shapers of clay and masters of wood and stone.
We are drummers of song and magicians of laughter.
Our hair, spiked with mud,
proclaims us astounding.

We find trees to shinny up and leap from
at fluttering aunts,
who come to fetch us from the creek
when neighbors complain.

We feel the world tremble
as they catalog our every monstrous deed—
our every gift to the gods of mud and summer.
Safe behind grandparents, who solemnly listen,
we peer around and call out our apologies.

16

But our grandma still loves us.
Our grandpa loves us, too.
Between kisses, we eat them up!
We put our beastie arms around their squishy middles
and *squeeeeeze.*

17

Oh, we are naughty ogres!
We run and shake our fannies at folks.
We sidle up to solemn big brothers,
to serious big sisters,
to soft-spoken elders,
and scratch mosquito bites, wipe noses,
pick at scabs on arms and legs.

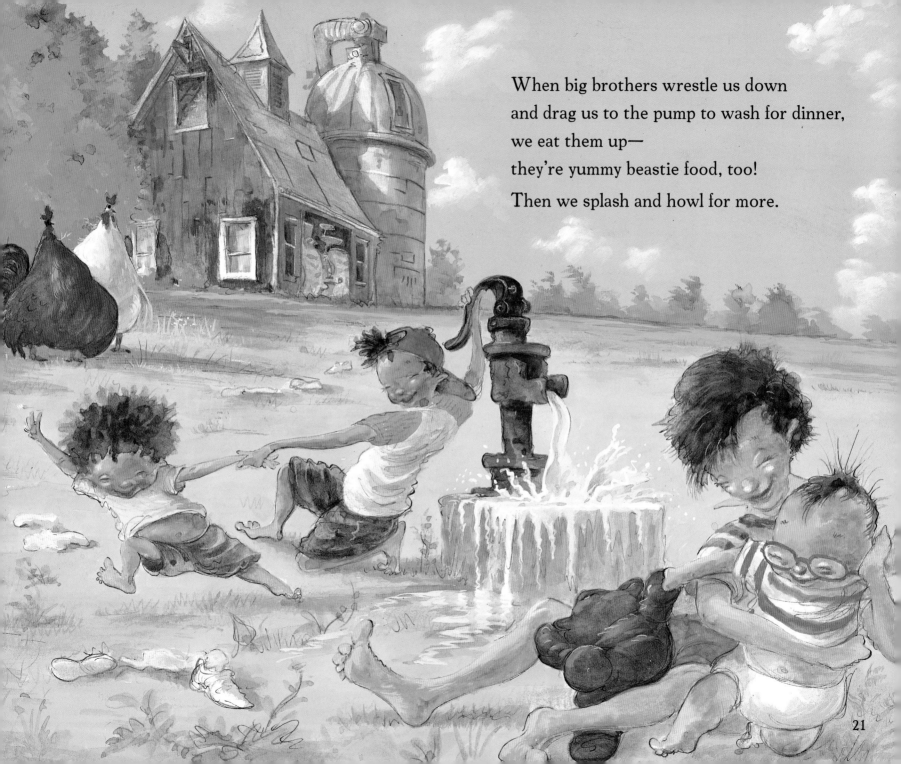

When big brothers wrestle us down
and drag us to the pump to wash for dinner,
we eat them up—
they're yummy beastie food, too!

Then we splash and howl for more.

21

Oh, we are hungry ogres!
Our dark eyes are aglint,
gazing at the hallowed tabletop.
We pile our plates high—a beastie feast—
pack tight together, and fidget,
longing to plunge our sharp teeth
into the sweet juiciness of the world.

As soon as heads are unbowed,
we eat and eat—and only stop to spit out seeds.

After dinner, we escape baths
given by big sisters,
throw undies out the window,
hide in the tall grass in our beastie jammies,
and jump out at stuffy busybodies.

Oh, we eat up the world!
We grab at moths and fireflies.
We fling ourselves, whirling,
beyond the crackling firelight
that spirals up to the stars,
stretching and pinching
our shadows off the earth.

By the time that coals are all that's left to glitter,
we're adrift in the murmuring river of adults.
Our bare feet drag through the settling dew.
We claw our way onto laps, steal hugs,
and snatch at splashes of song.

Oh, we are weary ogres!
We float, munching on tasty words
that well up in stories,
and on the soft lapping of laughter.
Ahhhhh, tender beastie food.

We sleep where we fall—
piled on dogs, spread-eagle in doorways,
draped over the strong shoulders of uncles.

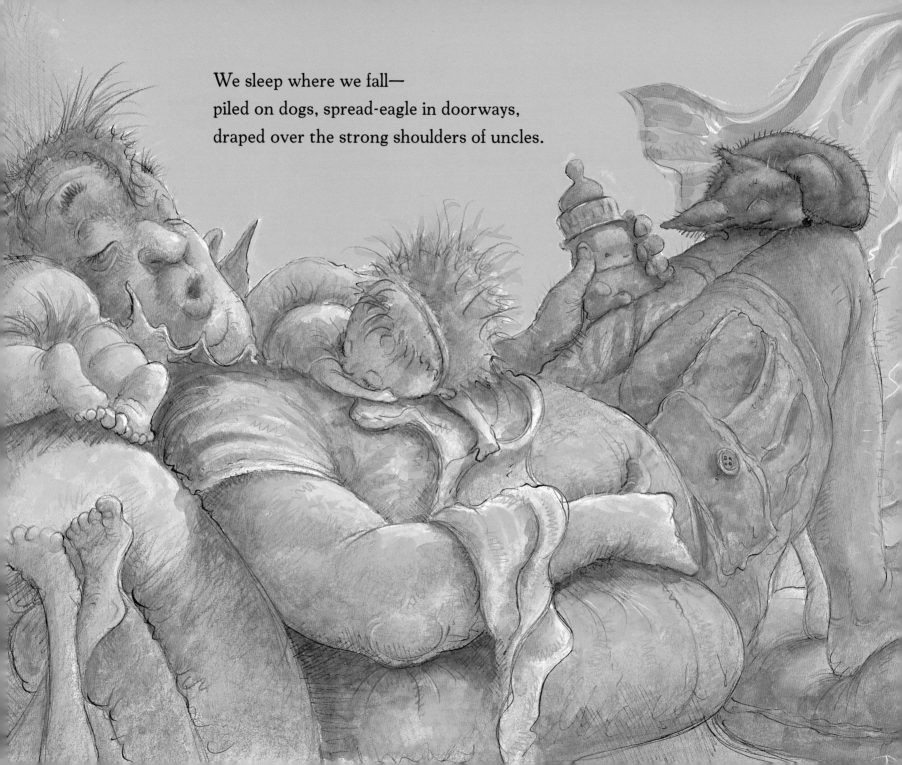

In the after-hush,
when some have left for home,
we are carried inside and sleep curled
amid arms and legs on pallets on the floor—
our grubby beastie toes pointing up
at the big open grin of the moon.

31

Oh, we are happy ogres, my cousins and I—
our hearts full, our tummies plump,
and our heads stuffed with dreams
of next year's beastie family reunion.